Hayride Fun

A First-Start® Easy Reader

This easy reader contains only 54 different words,
repeated often to help the young reader develop
word recognition and interest in reading.

a	cider	lots	there
after	doughnuts	misses	time
almost	farm	not	to
an	field	of	Tommy
and	fun	on	too
apple	get	our	tree
apples	going	pick	trees
are	hayride	pretending	trip
at	him	pull	wagon
be	horses	pumpkin	we
boo	in	pumpkins	where
bus	is	scarecrow	with
but	it	see	
can	look	the	

Hayride Fun

by Kristine Lombardi Frankel

illustrated by Cary Pillo

SCHOLASTIC INC.

New York Toronto London Auckland Sydney
Mexico City New Delhi Hong Kong Buenos Aires

ISBN 0-439-68799-3

12 11 10 9 8 7 6 5 4 3 2 1   4 5 6 7 8 9/0

Printed in the U.S.A.   08

First Scholastic printing, September 2004

We are going on a field trip.
Tommy almost misses the bus!

We are going on a field trip to a farm.
At the farm, we are going on a hayride!

There are pumpkins
and apples at the farm.
There are horses too.

We get in a wagon. But where is Tommy?
Tommy almost misses the hayride!

Horses pull the wagon.
We are going to the pumpkin field.

We see lots of pumpkins on the hayride.
We see apple trees too.
There is a scarecrow in the field!

We pick lots of apples.
Where is Tommy?
Tommy is in an apple tree!

We pick pumpkins too.
Where is Tommy?
Boo! Tommy is pretending
to be a scarecrow!

After the hayride, we get
apple cider and doughnuts.
But where is Tommy?

We look in the wagon.
But Tommy is not in the wagon.

We look in the apple trees.
But Tommy is not in an apple tree.

We look in the pumpkin field.
But Tommy is not with the pumpkins.

Where can Tommy be?
It is almost time to get on the bus.

Boo!
There Tommy is!

Tommy is pretending
to be a scarecrow.
But we can see it is him!

We get on the bus with
our apples and pumpkins.
Going on a hayride is lots of fun!